It's Bedtime

BY B. G. FORD

ILLUSTRATED BY ANTHONY RAO

A GOLDEN BOOK, NEW YORK
Western Publishing Company, Inc., Racine, Wisconsin 53404

 Library of Congress Catalog Card Number: 80-85081 ISBN 0-307-10112-6/ISBN 0-307-68112-2 (lib. bdg.)
MNOPQRST

Hurry up and finish your supper.
It's almost time for bed.

Go upstairs...

and take off your clothes...
and put them all away.

Brush your teeth...
and get ready for your bath.

Here are your boats and
your rubber duck.

It's time to stop playing
and start washing up.

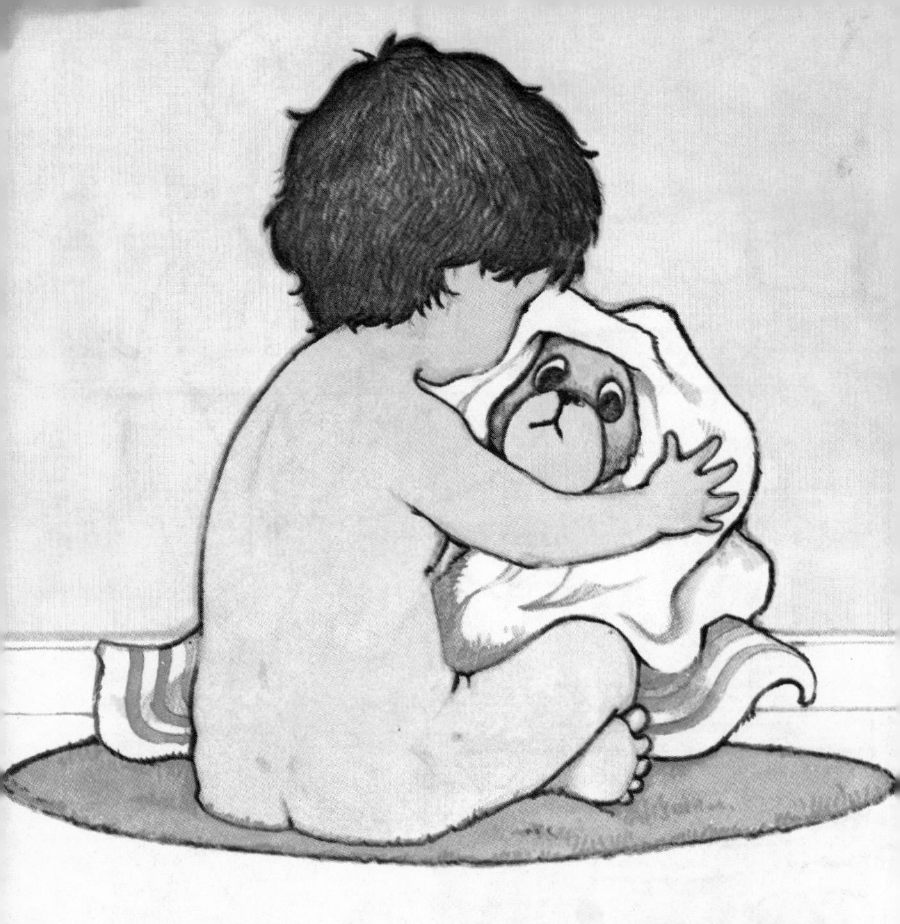

Out of the tub and dry yourself off.
It's almost time for bed.

Button up your nice warm pajamas.

Put away all your toys.

Would you like to
pick out a bedtime story?

That was a good story, wasn't it?
Let's read it over again.

It's Bedtime

Put the book back on the shelf.

Now it's time to say your prayers.

Climb into bed.

Yes, you may have just one sip of water.

It's time to turn out the light.

There, you're all tucked in.
Isn't it snuggly under the covers?

Good night.

Sleep tight.